To my friend Kuldip and all the other girls
who dream of exploring the stars

First U.S. edition 2019
First published by Otter-Barry Books (United Kingdom) 2019

Library of Congress Catalog Card Number 2019938934
ISBN 978-1-5362-0946-4

19 20 21 22 23 24 TLF 10 9 8 7 6 5 4 3

Printed in Dongguan, Guangdong, China

This book was typeset in Agenda.
The illustrations were done in acrylic.

Candlewick Press
99 Dover Street
Somerville, Massachusetts 02144

visit us at www.candlewick.com

ASTRO GIRL

Ken Wilson-Max

CANDLEWICK PRESS

Astrid had loved the stars and space ever since she could remember.

"I want to be an astronaut," Astrid told her best friend, Jake, as they gazed up at the stars.

"Will you bring me an asteroid when you come back from space?" asked Jake.

"Of course I will, Jakey."

"I want to be an astronaut!" Astrid said at breakfast.

"Are you sure?" Papa asked. "You'll have to go round and round the Earth in your spaceship."

He swung her around.

"I can do that," Astrid said, giggling.

"OK, Astro Girl, you'll also have to get used to zero gravity."

Papa threw her up in the air.

"I can do that all day long!"
Astrid laughed.

"Will a space cadet like you be able to sleep on your own among the stars?" Papa asked.

"I think that will be very hard . . . but I'll do it!" Astrid whispered.

At the space center,
Astrid and her papa
moved to the front of
the crowd just as the
doors opened.

"Mama!" Astrid gave her mama a big kiss.

"I missed you!" said Astrid.

"I want to be an astronaut, just like you," said Astrid. "You're my hero."

Astrid has learned a lot about being an astronaut:

The word *astronaut* comes from two Greek words: *astron,* meaning "star," and *nautes,* meaning "sailor."

American astronauts Neil Armstrong and Buzz Aldrin were the first to land on the moon, in the lunar module *Eagle,* on July 20, 1969.

The first animal to go into orbit was a dog named Laika, on the Russian Sputnik 2 spacecraft on November 3, 1957.

Valentina Tereshkova, from Russia, was the first woman in space, in 1963.

Shannon Lucid, from the United States, set an early record for the longest time spent in space by a woman (188 days in 1966).

Mae Carol Jemison was the first African-American woman in space, in 1992.

Helen Sharman was the first British astronaut and the first woman to visit the Mir space station, in 1991.

Kalpana Chawla was the first woman born in India to go to space, in 1997.

Space food is freeze-dried so that it won't spill and cause any damage to machines. Fruit, bread, and nuts are OK as they are.

Astronauts train underwater to create the feeling of floating in space.